MW01106550

The Mercenaries Of Havenshaw Crypt

The Mercenaries of Havenshaw Crypt is giddily published in the US and A by MorbidbookS and the Grace of God. Copyright: D.G. Sutter for words and music 2015. Cover Art by J.M. Cooper and poorly edited by Steven Scott Nelson, 2015. Stage direction by The Grim Reverend Steven Rage. The moral right, such as it is, of this author and his various disjointed proclivities have been asserted. All Rights Reserved. No part of this novella may be reproduced or transmitted in any form or by any electronic, alien or mechanical means including photocopying, recording, drawing stick figures, seventeenth century printing press, chain mail, or by any information storage and retrieval system, without the express written permission of The Reverend, D.G. Sutter, The Great and Powerful Oz and the Hand that turns the Big Wheel, except where permitted by law or whatever the hell you think you can get away with. But if you do, please be advised that you will incur the righteous disdain of The Reverend. And that is *no bueno, primo.* The characters in this vicious tome are fictitious. Duh. Obviously. Any resemblance to real persons, be they living or dead, demons, succubae, demi-gods or the 'formerly living' (zombies) is purely coincidental.

D.G. SUTTER

THE MERCENARIES OF

HAVENSHAW CRYPT

By

D.G. SUTTER

For

MorbidbookS is a grotesque Bizarro ballet where the most profane things occur. An impious and perverse dwelling of dark revulsion. A cozy cottage where torture porn and brutal bible tales are devised. A quiet place to relax and spin tales of depravity and wickedness. A halfway house for the disturbed where rules no longer apply. A safe haven for deviant serial killers to hatch their wretched schemes. Bring your pets. The tasty ones are always welcome.

WWW.MORBIDBOOKS.WORDPRESS.COM

CHAPTER 1

"MY CHILDREN ARE sleeping, there's little to do. I'm blinded by darkness, my vision askew."

The man in the rocking chair repeated this over and over, silently arcing forward, the slight breeze from the supports making the flame atop the white pillar candle dance as it sat on the round table. A shadow was sleeping in the corner, but when one of its limbs shifted, the rocking chair stopped abruptly. The father of the children sat forward, leaning into the wan light.

"Shhh..." he said, putting one bony-knuckled hand to his lips. His eyeballs swam lazily beneath the flaps of skin sewn shut with black thread.

The shadow tried to move again and the father jumped to his unsteady feet. "I said *shut the fuck up!*"

Finally, the shadow blended in with the darkness, creeping across the walls as if not there at all, irresolute in form. Satisfied, Father Necrocious laid his head against the back of the rocker.

"My children are sleeping, there's little to do. I'm blinded by darkness, my vision askew."

Using one shaky hand, Necrocious grabbed the decanter off the small mahogany table and pulled the cork out with a trying effort. His left hand he doused in the salty water, rubbing the liquid over his forehead, heart, and then his loins. Off the floor of the crypt, he grabbed a handful of ash and dirt and gently tossed it over the flame of the candle. His spine cracked when he sat upright.

After whispering his chant once more Necrocious fell to sleeping, barely a snore or sound escaping his throat. He did not witness the shadows as they began to break apart, or when they fully separated into silhouettes of trolls, demons, sprites, and other vile creatures. He did not witness the shadows as they tipped over the pillar candle and flames took to the walls. Then, the shadows seeped into the sand surrounding Necrocious's feet and vanished forevermore.

BENEATH THE GROUND——far, far in the depths of the pure soil——the lid of a splintered casket opened. A black hand shot through the side, shards of wood scraping by the appendage, dirt dipping under the cardboard fingernails. The body compressed and slipped through the opening in the box. It manipulated itself so as to sift between clumps of dirt and rocks that blocked its advance.

The thing was bothered by the hard ceiling at the surface, which to most was actually a floor. It knocked and banged, flimsy limbs catapulting off the ceiling-floor, digging a wide trench. The form expanded to full capacity and stretched as fast as possible, blasting a manhole sized access point.

There were stars above, resting on a map of deep blue. The black suited form sprung out of the hole and landed on the solid piece of land. Looking down at where he stood, Carbie knew he was born once more.

SPIKE WAS READY to get moving. He'd been curled like a snake around the branch of the tree so long that he could no longer stand it. Finally, he was awake and just needed to stay put and wait, but for how long? How long would it take for his brothers to arrive?

He poked one of his aluminum arms through a bushel of grapes and dropped it into the can by his feet. From around his waist, he uncoiled the long strand of metal, which at first look one would assume to be a belt, but was actually his penis.

"Fuck it," he said. "Piss wine, here I come."

How long, he wondered, since last a long, hot piss had passed through his pipes? Ten years? Fifteen, even? Once the pitter-patter of steamy liquid stopped Spike dove skyward, retracted his limbs into once fine, straight point, and started to stab the grapes in the can until they were mush.

It looked delicious when he was done. The once stringy red grapes, all veiny and rounded, were well blended to make a stellar pink concoction. Spike took the can in his thin hand. At the bottom was half of a cigarette. He laid it out to dry on the piece of volcanic rock near the tree's base.

"Smoke that later."

He then walked to the edge of the island and looked out at the sea of clouds. The only interruption was the skinny, and seemingly endless, piece of rock on which his island was balanced. Day time was creeping up, plastering light through the powdery clouds. When would they be here?

He took a long swig of the drink. The piss tasted great passing through his syphon lips. He could drink the shit all day. Hell, he may need to produce a subsequent batch. His brothers were always late.

IT WAS A quiet evening. Megamouth was sitting in his living room in the stomach of Mount Pus, when the walls began to rumble. He didn't think much of it, but still looked up from his text on volcanic insects in time to see his collection of germ wings crash toward the igneous floor. The scream he let out came from the bottom of his lungs. The sound vibrations funneled out of his pyramidal mouth, which jutted off of his face, and lifted the frame aloft of the floor.

He pulled the bark frame into his chest with both hands, triple knuckled fingers curling over opposing corners. Before he had a chance to move, the fleshy walls pulsed and squeezed. Pressure forced into his ears and channeled out his megaphone mouth, making the television explode, the flower vase shatter. He was shot into the air.

The passage he was pushed through felt like a long vagina, narrow and squishy. He shot into the tropical night, covered in Mount Pus's filthy yellow, protective juices.

When he landed, there were no clues giving away his position. The only thing he knew was that the glass on his germ collection was cracked and his brown wool suit coat was stained the color of boogers. Luckily, the wings he'd molded of his own dried feces slowed his descent. They were made for such an occasion as when Mount Pus would erupt. However, he wasn't prepared and was sent in a dizzying whirl through the air. If deployed a moment later he may not have survived.

He tried to breathe, but his mouth was clogged. The only air he could muster into his chunky body infused through his zucchini sized nose that rested atop the megaphone through which he spoke. He blew air through his nose and swallowed at the same time. Something traveled down his windpipe. He shrugged it off for the ability to breathe had returned.

Surrounding him was a ring of six giant wooden cubes. On each side of the blocks was a door, thirty six of them in all and no two the same. Some had odd shapes laid into the wood of the door, while others were very plain-looking bedroom-style entrances. Megamouth tapped into his intuition and felt a severe sense of urgency to his left. He walked in choppy steps, slightly dragging his left foot.

The aura was drifting downward and he could

feel it stronger across his head and shoulders than across his stomach. He reached toward the top of the cube, but couldn't reach. Thus, he was forced to flap his fecal wings. The door on the plane perpendicular to the sky was the one emitting the feeling. He tried the handle made of pure pewter and linked like a chain fence. The handle flapped limply, only giving resistance.

Unable, as usual, to control the volume of his voice, Megamouth shouted: **"OPEN UP!"**

The door did not oblige. It was denying him entry and therefore pissing him off royally. He dug into his pants pocket and found the multi-tool he carried everywhere. Many attachments branched off of the tool——a toaster oven that unfolded from a toothpick, a gumball machine that only needed water to grow—— but none as useful and fanciful as the candid can opener.

After flicking the switch the curved point of the attachment began metamorphosis. The point rounded into a head, from the squared sides there branched two arms, and the base detached into two scrawny legs, melding from the corners. The tool Megamouth once more pocketed, but the can opener he held in his massive palm, awaiting the finality of the transformation.

When finally the small can opener man began to move of his own volition——clawing across Megamouth's hands, etching deep wounds——he placed the daemon on top of the door. Rufus, as Megamouth had come to call him, dragged his two inch body toward the dangling keyhole near the knob. He was still unable to speak, but remembering how to mobilize his throat muscles always took a little longer.

The lock clicked when Rufus started to dig around inside the hole and the door fell into the frame. Megamouth started to fall and grabbed the two inch daemon in passing, placing Rufus on his shoulder. Far below was a world of clouds, beyond which he could not see a thing. He closed his eyes, terrified of the splat below. His scream resonated through the megaphone, so loud that it damaged his own ears. Blood trickled out of his right canal. He could smell it with his giant schnoz.

A tiny whisper could be heard over the rush of the air. *"Quiet down!"*

Then, Rufus found his voice and yelled: **"FLY, SHIT WINGS!"**

CHAPTER 2

IT FELT LIKE he'd been waiting for days when really it was only eight hours or so. Being brought back to a state of animation meant that his father was still alive. Unfortunately, it most likely meant that his father had not accomplished their mission. Spike knew his choice order of business, but it would have to wait for a conference between children and father. A great deal of persuasion would be needed to sway his father, but Spike had manipulation down, especially regarding his very dim brother. He was an easy vote.

Spike finished off two batches of piss wine and was waiting for the urge to sting before he could make another, when movement caught his eye. A clambering black form had breached the mass of marshmallow clouds. Spike squinted, his round brown eyes barely hanging onto his needle-thin face. The form's arms were wrapped around the skinny base that held the island in place, so high up in the air. It was his brother, Carbie.

He rejoiced by pumping his hand in the air, for it was true. His brother was en route, scaling the vertical piece of land. Spike lay on the grass beneath the grape vines and peeked over the edge. What Spike lacked was Carbie's strength, his ability to plow through people or walls. Spike was great at manipulation, both physical and mental. He always thought that maybe his mental traits were stolen from his youngest brother's gene pool, the big dumb fuck. *Maybe father dipped into his test tube*, Spike thought.

Carbie scuttled up the base and then, reaching the bottom of the island, burst through the ground. The ground shook and the leaves on the tree rustled. When he landed there was a cracking sound and the island teetered. Spike remained perfectly still on his back, aware that his brother's grand entrance had disrupted the island-in-the-cloud's stability. Carbie also stood stock-still in his spandex suit, breaths frequently expanding and compressing his chest.

"Don't move," Spike said in his metallic voice.

"I'm not."

"Where's the loud mouth?"

"He's not with me, obviously," Carbie said. "Do you know where he was last seen?"

Spike cackled. "If I did, would I be asking you?"

"No."

They remained motionless and quiet for some time, worried the island would break off and fall through the sky. When it became clear that the third brother was going to be further late, a decision needed to be made. After such a long tenure in complete stillness, neither of them wanted to endure it a second longer. Both understood the gravity of the situation (and how couldn't they?), being so experienced in dire circumstances.

"I'll slither over the edge," Spike said. "Then, I'll

slowly climb onto the support."

"Be careful."

He'd been waiting for the supplication and when it came, Spike wrapped two hands full of pin sharp fingers into the underside of the island. There was another sharp "crack!" and he halted progress.

"Steady...steady," Carbie said.

"I'm good," Spike said. "I'm a skinny bastard, unlike you. You're the one that's got to be careful where you walk."

"Why's that?"

"You're a bag of shit. Everyone knows that. You're a thousand times recycled."

Carbie blew a raspberry, his corrugated tongue flapping in the wind.

"How far up are we?" Spike asked.

"About twenty thousand or so."

Carbie took a heavy step, starting to follow Spike without permission.

"Don't move another foot! It's unstable."

"I know what I'm doing."

He lifted his foot in the air. If Spike could see Carbie's face beneath the tight black hood, he assumed it would be adorned with a box-cutter-forged smile. The brother dropped his square foot onto the dirt, tipping the can of piss wine into the grass. The island started to tilt downward. Spike's body became vertical. Carbie stood on an opposing horizontal axis to the ground.

The half-cigarette flipped out of the piss wine, falling past Spike's face, spattering his cheeks with stale urine and squished grapes. He unlatched one of his hands in time to stab through the filter and then jammed it back into the dirt, securing the smoke under his hand.

"Nice knowing you, Carbie!" he yelled over the rush of air.

Carbie's mouth was moving. Spike could see a brown hole through the slit in his hood, but could not hear him. He looked over his shoulder. The clouds were approaching at an alarming rate.

Oh boy, he thought. *This is it.*

The Mercenaries Of Havenshaw Crypt

They entered the fields of clouds and Spike expected to feel them brushing his metal parts like cotton, but was disappointed when they merely dissipated in retaliation. The hope had been to taste them like whipping on a cake, but then, he didn't taste anything but the screaming wind, drying out his mouth.

Then, the clouds all but disappeared. He looked over his shoulder. The ground was visible, maybe a mile below. A range of extremely close together mountain peaks, thousands and thousands like the bottom of a mountainside comb, sat as a death trap. The piece of land that had been holding the island grew out of the very center of the range, a massive flagpole.

He tried to reach behind his head and stab into the strip, but couldn't quite reach. When finally he did, the force ripped his arm away, bent it over the edge of the island like a candy cane.

It seemed as though all options were abandoned. However, as Spike conceded to defeat, hoping maybe to land unscathed amongst the peaks and valleys, a beacon of hope shone. Floating below was a familiar hulk wearing brown wings. He hoped the loud mouth would see them in time.

The brown wings flapped, spinning the brother in circles, oblivious to the island rapidly descending upon him. Spike didn't try to warn him, for he would not have been able to hear it. Instead, he dropped silently, crossing his metal fingers.

With mere seconds to spare the imbecile lifted his head, apparently not hearing the sound of a giant rock breaking the aero-dynamic barrier. His circular eyes widened and his funnel mouth pulsed. Spike wasn't prepared for the onslaught of noise. His ear canals were penetrated by the low embrace of a spectacular foghorn.

Megamouth's scream derived from fright, it was not meant to levitate the island. Yet, it sent the rock spinning in barrel rolls and Spike saw Carbie flip off the surface.

He screamed: *"Noooooo!"* But his cry was lost on the wind.

In the dizzying flips he saw the ground pass by numerous times, as well as the sight of his youngest brother frantically attempting to fly beneath the island. Then, Megamouth was humming, at a much calmer level, and the island was gravitated by his voice. The ride took longer than it would have if the island dropped all the way to the mountains, but Spike counted his blessings once the piece of land holding the tree and grape vines landed gently in a gulley. He lit his piss-drunk smoke.

CHAPTER 3

"WHAT THE HELL you got there?" Spike asked Megamouth first thing. He was holding a frame crafted of bamboo.

"Deez my germ wings. Found them in Pus Mountain," he yelled.

"So why'd you bring them here? You know we have things to do."

Megamouth scratched his ass. His red bow tie was crooked. Rufus whispered into his ear. Then he responded "Dey my prized possession."

Spike sighed. He'd brought the little smart ass with him. "Tell Rufus to mind his own business, would ya'?"

The daemon stood on Megamouth's shoulder, wearing an identical sports jacket and slacks, pulled his wiener out and gave Spike the finger at the same time. He then sat down on his perch and kicked his feet like a munchkin from Oz.

"Whatever," Spike said. "You ready to get back home?"

Megamouth nodded, his gigantic nose shaking like a flaccid penis. "Home, home. I'm ready for home." His last word echoed as it vacated his megaphone, as if it was the only thing in the world he wanted——to go home.

Spike hurried ahead like a gazelle, while Megamouth lumbered far behind, trying to keep pace. He loved his little brother, would always look out for him, but Spike was often annoyed by him, too. Thus, he allowed him to lag while talking to the friend on his shoulder, and talk he did.

"What about Carbie?" Megamouth yelled out as they progressed.

Spike hoped Carbie was okay, but they couldn't waste any time looking for him. Too much time had already lapsed while waiting. If he was alive, he'd find a way home. He was a grown man. "He'll find us."

CARBIE LANDED AND broke apart, boxes flying through the treetops and sliding into the swamp. He could feel each and every part, not only the pieces connected to his central processing box, but those scattered through the forest. It took hours for him to coax his parts to return. One particular scrap, maybe a cereal box lid that was part of his eyebrow, just would not cooperate. It lounged in the orange stream, basking in bacterial sweetness.

He finally decided to leave it behind and bunched into his tattered and torn spandex suit. It was unfortunate to be trapped in the forest alone, for he knew the place belonged to Colonel Brimstone——one of his father's archenemies——who rode around the forest with his troupe of elephant riders, kidnapping trespassers. Children were shrunk per order of the current Dictator (who last Carbie knew was Manservant Genesis), and held until the Dictator's Ball. Adults were burnt alive, taken as food for Ignatius the Ape and his Tremulous Tribe, or sacrificed.

Father was adamant about turning his enemies to shadows, despite such vicious practices, but hopefully things were soon to change. Carbie was starting to believe in his brother Spike's philosophy that more desperate action was necessary. After the last attempt to overturn the band of Dictators, they only captured Manservant Genesis and some of his trolls. Since he and his brothers had inflicted so much damage, Father suspended their animation.

Carbie's ability to move slowly returned. First, he was walking at nothing more than a shuffle, but his strength grew and he graduated to a steady run, until he was dodging branches of trees and bushes that reached with thorny hands. In his swiftness, he passed a watching sentinel without noticing. The eyes lit up in the dark of the forest, red and vicious, and hurried off in a different direction.

IT WASN'T UNTIL Spike saw the white sign that he remembered where they were.

"All trespassers subject to shrinkage, imprisonment, or burning alive, without exception, per order of Colonel Brimstone."

Spike told Megamouth he'd be right back and sprang twenty feet in the air, latching onto the peak of a tree. For miles and miles around he could only see forest, and could not remember the direction of the Crypt. After uncoiling from around the trunk, he dropped to the floor of the thicket, his two ridiculously sharp feet stabbing in like tent stakes.

"Damn it, loud mouth."

"What's wrong?"

He shook his head, "Only trees. I don't see any way out of this place."

Though they could endeavor into the woods, if they encountered Brimstone a provocation would occur.

Spike wasn't concerned about losing a fight, but wasn't sure he could practice discretion and shadowtize Brimstone. Shadows had a way of sneaking off and becoming very troublesome.

"Guess our options are limited," Spike said. "We go through the forest."

However, as they started to walk away, Spike was startled by his loud mouth brother.

"Oh, oh, oh! Oh, wait!"

Spike turned towards the behemoth. "What?"

Rufus cupped his tiny hands around Megamouth's ears, whispering a secret. The giant brother stupidly shook his head, his mouth hanging open.

"Remember? Me have shit wings! I can fly us home."

The frame was still gripped in his hands, a large crack cutting it down the middle.

"What about your collection?"

Megamouth looked down at the frame that was nestled into his chest. He removed one of his hands and started to dig through his pocket. His hand reappeared holding an item that looked like a larger Swiss Army knife.

"Watch my new tool!"

The massive brother bent over and gently placed the frame on the ground. Rufus nearly fell of his shoulder, at the last moment grabbing his owner's lapel.

Megamouth opened the tool, flipping an appendage that looked like a flashlight. He pressed a button on the side and a suctioning sound began. The frame warped, expanded, shrank until it was small as a cherry, and then vanished inside of the tool.

"For safe's keeping!" he accidentally yelled.

Spike didn't know what to make of the tool. So far as he knew shrinking tools were exclusive to his father's professed enemies (five of the toughest creatures in the universe), known as the Flagrant Five.

"Where'd you get that?"

Megamouth stared, dumbfounded, at the device in his hand. Then, as if just remembering a question he was asked, snapped loudly "Me made it with bare hands!"

The behemoth showed his palms to Spike, all callused and worn, the skin peeling off. He was the only one of the brothers who'd had limited mobility, able to walk around within the belly of the volcano, Mount Pus. He was always Father's favorite. However, Spike wasn't sure of what he would have made the device. Where could he have possibly gotten the tools necessary?

"Ready to fly?" Megamouth asked.

Spike shook his head in amazement; sometimes his idiot brother truly surprised him. "As ready as I'm going to be."

Megamouth grabbed Spike around the thin waist, holding him with the sort of strength reserved for a body builder. Then, Spike could hear a flapping of wings and the ground began to fade. The forest ahead stretched for as far as the eye could see, just one mass of ceaseless evergreens. Spike coiled around Megamouth's hand, as an extra precaution. Though, he knew his Herculean brother would refuse to let him drop.

Spike tried his best to ignore the stench, but after

hours and hours of flying the smell began to wear Spike down. It was the reason he'd originally opted to walk when they landed in the forest. The breeze was stagnant and the only wind was created of the vile wings, directed straight downward toward Spike's face. Patience had always been one of his greatest virtues, but this most recent awakening seemed to have changed that.

Megamouth contained a sort of internal compass, intuiting him to certain places or things, but the trip seemed to be taking longer than necessary.

"How much farther, do you think?" Spike asked.

"Can't you see?" he bellowed, abruptly.

Sure enough, spread out on the horizon was the expansive Havenshaw Crypt, the cemetery for the entire world. It wouldn't be long before they were home to father, and able to discover why he'd awoken them. Hopefully, thought Spike, his father's position on the Flagrant Five could be changed. He really was ready to spill some blood.

CHAPTER 4

BEING SUCH A heavy mass, it was difficult for Carbie to tread lightly, but he tried to move as swiftly and quietly as possible. The forest was barren where it had once thrived with thousands of species. There had been Goltens (volcanic golems of a very gentle sort), Marchovies (troops of fish-headed men who were able to sustain on land and water), Barges (an unusually vicious creature made from litter), and even Piestols (fresh blueberry pie beasts able to launch rotten berries at predators).

Barges and Piestols had all but been killed off by Colonel Brimstone. The Marchovie and Golten populations were staggering and not much higher. There were other beautiful creatures of the forest as well, but they were forced to migrate. It made life easier, only having to worry about capture from Brimstone rather than falling prey to a creature, but was indeed a sad complication.

Carbie sliced away vines and branches using the sharp edges of his hands. Ten years before, just previous to the last stretch of sleep, he spent hours rubbing them against a whet stone, prepping to divorce Ignatius's head from his body. How he would have loved to slice it clean off like the big round end of a pepperoni stick, watch the fucker's blood spill like liquid candy from a piĐata.

He hacked through a sapling, dove, and tumbled over a fell tree. They grew up out of nowhere in seconds, died in days. It boggled Carbie's mind why the Five had never discovered a method of using the trees instead of shrinking children for their sick election. Could they not paint and carve the trees?

Yet, it was not up to Carbie. The Five had ruled the world for so long as anyone alive could remember. If it wasn't Manservant Genesis pushing people to join his side, it was Brimstone, or Ignatius. They were large and powerful, and no one possessed the ability to overtake them, including the brothers. It had long been their father's personal mission to turn them all to shadows and lock them away, restore order to the world. Carbie was starting to think the plan would never work.

Over the following hill Carbie was able to run much faster because of the widened trail. For one reason or another he was oblivious to the fact that trails don't typically expand so wide in the forest, because the trees grow in such expedition. He was also unaware to being hot on someone else's trail, unaware that ahead was a group who would've been more desirable to meet alongside his brothers. So, he continued on along the path of crushed bushes and mashed trees, grape vines devastated, and general destruction.

THEY'D FLOWN DIRECTLY over Colonel Brimstone's embargo. It took all that Spike had to remain levelheaded and to not have Megamouth drop him like a paratrooper into the woods. Instead they landed safely as a pair (trio if you included Rufus) on the grounds on Havenshaw Crypt. They passed the familiar grey, chipping sign outside of the stone wall and entered through the black metal door, which was held closed by three vertical clasps.

Inside, the lights were not ignited. So Spike cranked up his lighter and sparked the flint. He eased the flame toward the oil and the fire spread in a thin strip along the spanning walls, in both directions. The tunnels were equally vacant and gloomy as he remembered.

"Daddy!" Megamouth shouted, and it echoed through the narrow halls.

Spike slapped him with one metal hand. It accidentally stabbed through Megamouth's suit and into his plastic body.

"Ouch! What if I told on you?"

"Go for it," Spike replied.

He could smell sulfur and walked cautiously toward the staircase directly across from the entrance. Something didn't feel right. Something was completely amiss.

As they began to descend the wide stairwell, Spike could smell the stagnancy of an old candle, could see the snakes of smoke teasing the underground walls forged of skulls and bones. They seemed to be laughing at him, humored by his ignorance. His gait enhanced, worried for his father's safety. Megamouth lumbered behind, yelling for Spike to "Wait up!", but he didn't slow.

At the bottom of the long stairs the hall opened into the massive chamber filled with sarcophagi and coffins, and oddly... walking corpses. How, Spike marveled, were beasts and men who were supposed to be no longer alive, walking about the room? Father was the only one in the known universe with the power to summon the dead, and he would never have granted it *all* back. Almost every coffin was lidless. Mummies had broken the restraints of their sarcophagi and walked about unheeded.

Megamouth released a resounding "Wow!" when he happened upon the scene and Spike was again forced to slap the back of his plastic head. The dead lacked the capability to control emotion, due mostly to the deterioration of the mind, but also from their jealousy towards those who still could eat, breathe, and speak. It instilled the last sentient part of their brain to yearn for the destruction of that which they could never again attain.

"You loud mouth," Spike said, as the dead turned in unison to face them.

"Look what you've done. We're fucked. These assholes are going to tear us to pieces."

"Sorry. So sorry..."

"Don't be sorry. Just watch it! Let's move before they reach us."

Spike felt like a babysitter and a protector for his youngest brother sometimes. He was a terror to control, but when used correctly could destroy battalions, could menace an entire stronghold singlehandedly. Keeping him under your thumb was the extremely difficult part.

They treaded along the back wall of the chamber, skeletal arms reaching out from the border between leering skulls and bony legs, which tried to run. Being the largest room, and therefore containing the principal quantity of deceased, the two brothers were aware of the need to swiftly depart. Yet, the minions of the dead wanted no part in letting them escape. They shambled ever closer, some of them in rapid decay and their pace reflecting, others freshly dead and moving with the same exhilaration.

A group of creatures blocked the exit leading to Father's home. Spike readied for battle by bending his metal fingers into claws while he ran. They were thin, but sharp, and with enough force could tear through any materials, human, troll, Gary, or otherwise.

Speaking of Garys, he noticed a few of the dead were Garys. They were easy to pick out of a crowd, for they were all identical——black freckles, bushy brown hair, slightly green skin. Such an easily conquerable race thought Spike, easily controlled, easily manipulated, and easy to destroy if need be (especially dead ones).

Spike swam through the crypt air, between floating pieces of tissue and bacteria. His right hand ripped a Gary's arm off and flung it at another's head, which with due force tore free and splattered against a wall of compound bones. After he flipped over the pack and into the anticipating hall, he could see Megamouth pounding human bodies into Gary bodies, smashing them together like action figures, while wearing a look of determined anger. Rufus was gripping Megamouth's suit lapel, wearing a wide O-mouth.

"C'mon, hurry it up," Spike yelled through the melee.

Megamouth looked up, saw his brother waiting in the hall, and nodded. He swiveled in a circle, letting his megaphone blare the deafening cry of a foghorn. Heads exploded and bodies fell on top of each other, creating piles of rotting bloody corpses. One of the fell

Garys tried to grab Megamouth's foot, but he accidentally stepped on the things skull, crushing it like a walnut.

"Oops!" he cried.

They made haste down the following stairwell, finally reaching the door to their father's home, where they'd all been crafted and grown. Spike opened the door.

The inside was dark and charred. There was no light or shadows. The walls were burnt completely and Spike marveled the small wooden house—— constructed inside of the crypt——had not collapsed. Father was nowhere to be seen. Since he was no longer present in the Crypt, it was the reason the dead could re-animate. It also meant that Manservant Genesis was free.

CHAPTER 5

HE HADN'T HEARD them coming, hadn't seen the cage

falling, but sure enough Carbie was captured. The material encasing his body was not something Carbie ever encountered. He slammed against the bars, but they were reinforced so that his cardboard arms bounced right off.

The sentinels stood guard outside the cage, looking in with their arms crossed. Their red eyes glowed darkly in their sockets, which were carved into wolven faces. These were the keepers of the forest, paid with blood by Colonel Brimstone. They were deathly silent and moved with such grace Carbie hadn't time to react.

One minute he was chugging along on the outskirts of the forest (he could actually see the boundaries) the next he was caged up like an animal. Worst of all, was the silence as they stood there. They spoke no words, simply eyeballed him. He could hear the one they answered to headed his way——the pounding footsteps, the falling trees, the roar of the ensuing flames.

The trees in line with his vision swayed

powerfully before falling. He could have been wrong, but Carbie sensed the slight hint of a smirk on the sentinels' faces as the broad side of a giant grey animal came into sight. Colonel Brimstone led the pack, drowning the forest with his flamethrower in passing. Trees took to flame and he cackled in response, the inconsiderate prick.

Even across the distance, Carbie could see the gap between his teeth, could see the perspiration on his monocle, dripping down into his handlebar mustache. He pulled the trigger on the flamethrower and shot fire into the branches, tilting his head back and cackling as the flames poured free of the gun. They engulfed one of the Colonel's men and he fell free of his elephant, scorching the side of the beast. Its trunk swung wantonly back and patted out the fire spreading on its leathery back, unflinching, as if it'd happened a thousand times before. Brimstone pointed at the flailing, screaming body, still rolling with laughter and disrespect.

He held his hand into the air, *"Stop!"*

The riders pulled on their reigns and some of the elephants reared. Once the group settled——and the only noise the ocean of fire, spreading through the greens——Brimstone swung off his animal and landed softly on the ground. The sentinels spread out, vanishing back into the woods on his approach. Carbie crossed his arms in an attempt to feign fearlessness. However, he couldn't feel sure of himself without his brothers.

Brimstone slung the gun behind his back so that only the strap crossed over his chest. From his right side he withdrew a whip, which had been hooked under his belt. The tails of the weapon cracked over Carbie's cheek, sending the pile of cardboard into the bars behind.

"Ah, what a fool, what a fool," Brimstone muttered beneath his frilly mustache. "Now why, pray tell, would you be wandering around my forest?"

"Just passing through..."

"Oh, don't play coy, Carbie. Where are you headed?"

Carbie snickered beneath his hood.

The whip snapped over his neck and Carbie could feel the boxes collapse. His head lolled onto one shoulder.

"Havenshaw Crypt, I presume. Seems you won't be making it there. Even so, I've gotten word from my sentinels that Manservant Genesis is back from the shadows...headed for the Dictator's Ball."

Colonel Brimstone turned and started towards his elephant. The creature grabbed the eight foot tall man in its trunk and gently placed him on its back.

"Bring him along!" Brimstone ordered.

His ride stomped past the cage, rattling the bars, and Carbie wished he could get his hands on the Colonel. If it was possible, he wouldn't waste time with a shadow gun per his father's wishes. He would eliminate the bastard.

Two of his followers ran to the cage and began hooking chains to the bars. He could see the patterns on their skin, red and blue cross-hatching, as if someone's grandmother had quilted them. Unlike Brimstone, they were short and plump, smaller than Carbie.

They were just within reach. He slid his two square arms through the bars and crushed their wind pipes. Their heads exploded and cotton stuffing blew out from all four ears. The quilted minions collapsed in a craftsy heap. The other followers began to scream and Carbie saw they also carried miniature versions of Brimstone's flamethrower.

One of the uncontrolled elephants charged for the cage. There was no other choice for Carbie but to curl into a ball. The cage was lifted and thrown into a tree. Carbie heard a loud crack and when he landed, the broken cage scattered around his body. He barely regained his bearings in time to dodge a trampling. The animal went careening into the forest, taking out trees and stomping bushes and saplings into nothing.

Carbie rolled across the sod, coming up in between another passing elephant's legs. The animal reared in fear and threw the rider from his saddle. The rider was stepped on by the next elephant in line and squished into a pile of stuffing on its sole. Carbie wasn't quite on his feet when the hail of fire fell upon him from the sky.

His shoulder caught and he dropped to the ground, tossing dirt on the flames. Cardboard being so flammable, he was very lucky to have doused it so fast. The rider spewing fire was Brimstone. The Colonel circled around and was directly upon him. It was odd to see the others continuing on the path unguided, as if Brimstone wanted a piece of Carbie himself. Fire came rushing toward his face and Carbie dove under the elephant. The animal started to spin in circles.

Carbie rolled one nylon sleeve up and sliced his corrugated hand across the elephant's leg. It was the most painful type of cut, deep and stinging, inflicted by recycled waste. Brimstone's ride trumpeted and rushed into the trees, but the Colonel executed a beautiful backflip off the animal, landing in a perfect stance.

As the Colonel raised his flamethrower, Carbie pulled his shadow pistol out of its holster. The piece reminded him of his brothers and their mission. He realized Spike was right all along. Turning the Five to shadows was in ineffective. Somehow they always found an escape. Something needed to drastically change.

The fire arced through the woodland air, scorching hanging branches and roasting the dust right out of the sky. Carbie booked toward where the crushed quilted minion, for his flame thrower lay discarded. Heat teased Carbie's heels. He could feel impending death by incineration.

His thick hand snagged the strap of the weapon and he flipped it into his hands. Pulling the trigger was cathartic. It fulfilled every deep desire. Carbie and Brimstone's flames connected at the center, but when the fire disbanded and the smoke cleared there stood a much crisper version of Brimstone, charred and blackened. His mustache crumbled off his lip like the crust of overcooked toast.

THE HALL WAS full of the dead. Spike counted thirteen Garys alone packed into the doorframe. He couldn't imagine what was waiting beyond. With a somersault through the air, he removed four of their heads using each of his pointed limbs as weapons. Putrid blood splashed over the squirming walls and inside of Megamouth's megaphone. The brother spit frantically, trying to release the acrid liquid, and wound up screaming at the top of his lungs. The reverberation knocked Spike through the Crypt, toppling mummies, trolls, and unidentifiable corpses. It wasn't his intention to clear a path out of the crypt, but he had nonetheless.

A troll died a second time as it staggered to its

feet and one of the bony arms shot out of the wall, tearing its head clean off of its green and warty shoulders.

Before, they weren't avoiding the walls, but Spike really wanted his head to stay where it was. As they rushed parallel to the wall on the left, the dead stumbled past the support pillars as a mass. The army was closing in. The left turn into the stairwell leading to the surface seemed like an easy accomplishment, but was too good to be true. The dead were packed shoulder to shoulder in the dim and narrow enclosure.

"Uh-oh," Megamouth said.

For a bunch of supposed dead they sure radiated with excess energy, thought Spike. They clawed pieces off one another, tearing limbs free to make way for their own advance.

Spike rolled his neck. "Looks like it's time to get to work," he said.

Megamouth looked dumbfounded, but that was nothing new. He plucked Rufus off his shoulder and placed him lightly on the ground. The loud mouth dug into his suit jacket, pulled out the multi-tool, and placed it in the two inch thing's outstretched hands.

"No… he'll take care of it."

Rufus twisted the tool and rested it on his tiny shoulder, barely able to stand burdened with the weight.

"He can barely hold the thing," Spike said. "What is he going to do?"

The small man, beast (Spike still wasn't quite sure what he was or where he came from) mouthed "eat shit" and scuttled toward the stairwell. The tiny creature became a flash of intermittent grey, shooting from corpse to corpse, destroying reanimates in milliseconds. Spike was nearly amazed, but had seen better shows from warriors. Yet, for his size, Rufus had done quite a job. The bodies were piled atop of one another, like rows of fell dominoes.

The only exit was past the rug of corpses. So, they trampled over the stinking and decaying bodies. Spike's foot dug into an abdomen. He pulled it out covered in rotten tissue and goo. The shockingly active dead were creeping and moaning behind the troupe, easing into the stairwell. Spike reached back, over Megamouth's shoulder, and stabbed through one half-decomposed eye.

His brother yelped in surprise and the sound waves wafted Spike to the top of the stairs, where he rolled and slammed against the wall. Skeletal hands gripped his entire body. Bony knees and heels pulsed into his back and spine, manipulating his parts in directions they weren't meant to move. One of his arms twisted in a most unnatural manner, bending his elbow in the reverse direction.

Megamouth lumbered up the stairs just as Spike became wholly confined against the wall of marrow. His younger brother was exceptionally concerned, per the look upon his face, and rightfully so. Megamouth's thick plastic hands clenched into eight inch squares and he swung a giant right fist into the wall above Spike's body.

The pin-thin brother closed his eyes as shards of bone rained down. The grip on his right shoulder relieved and he dug his hand into the sodden floor over and over, clawing away from the bones. Wide-eyed

Megamouth furrowed his brows in anger and pounded away at the brittle imprisoners. Spike rolled away from the wall and vaulted to his feet. A tiny form charged toward them from the top of the stairs and Spike had a mind to kick the tiny daemon back into the largest Crypt. If only it wasn't his little brother's best friend, he thought.

Rufus leapt from the ground and landed on Megamouth's shoulder. He took a seat on the massive boulder of plastic and whispered into his owner's ear. Megamouth shook his head intently while nodding.

"He says...no more of them. They sleeping now."

Being the skeptic, Spike gazed down the corridor. Sure enough, there was no movement.

"Holy crap," he whispered under his breath.

The bottom entrance to the crypt was completely blocked by a pile of corpses——wall to wall decomposition.

"Now what we do?" asked Megamouth. "Daddy's gone. He dead."

Spike didn't have a plan. It was true that father

was either dead or kidnapped. He supposed the latter to prove true, for if Father Necrocious was dead much more pandemonium would be at hand.

"We have to find out what happened to him," Spike said, turning to face his brother. "I don't think he's dead, but I think Manservant Genesis might be clued in to his location."

Megamouth cowered. On their last encounter, Manservant cracked his brother's back down the middle. Spike could still hear the howls of pain when he fell to the ground. In order to reach Manservant they'd have to pass directly through the marketplace, chancing a fight with Lady Moreover and her despicable twin, Porticus Labary. Yet, Spike didn't know where else to start.

CHAPTER 6

THE ELEPHANT RIDERS pursued him for hours. Carbie hid in tight spaces and climbed vertical cliffs to escape.

He incinerated two of the riders with the flamethrower, but was forced to leave it behind while he swam through a lake. It was worth the loss, for despite their riders' pleas the elephants were reluctant to move into the frigid waters.

It seemed Carbie had escaped when he landed on the opposing shore away from the pursuers, with one of the Flagrant Five (well... now Four) a pile of ashes. However, he forgot one precious reminder. Being made of cardboard was not an attribute conducive for swimming. So, despite his achievement in escaping the prosecution, his body was thoroughly saturated by the heavy water.

He lay on the edge of the lake in a heap on the sand. His arms and legs were soggy and unwilling to give him the needed support. At least while swimming they worked as paddles, though quite sluggish ones. On land he had no sense of structure. He was a pile of shit. With the lack light for drying he realized it could take hours, or even days, until he aired out enough to reform.

The sun had since dropped from the sky, letting

a blanket of darkness comfort him. He closed his eyes, hoping his brothers would come to the rescue before the elephant riders could traverse the lake's circumference. Carbie dreamt of the Crypt, of how he was traveling in the opposite direction with no other choice. He dreamt of seeing his father. It'd been such a stretch deprived of contact.

Long gone were the days when they (meaning the brothers, the mercenaries) roamed the land, uninterrupted. They could no longer subsist by following bounties. Father loved them, but deemed them menaces, took away their freedoms. So what if they killed for a paycheck? They always listened (well, most of the time) when it came down to the Five. For one reason or another father wanted the Five to remain unharmed. Despite his disgust for their roulette wheel of dictatorship, he always ordered the brothers to turn the assholes into shadows instead of murdering them. It was silly. They made the world a terrible place in which to live.

Carbie fell fast asleep. His subconscious gears

continued to spin the semantics of the world, but his body didn't exhibit much activity. Occasionally, the wind would push the water toward his body, further soaking him, but other than that he was still. He was a pile of pasta, soaking in an unnecessary pool, becoming overcooked.

Daylight broke without Carbie opening his eyes. The elephant riders never found him, but without Brimstone they probably became lost within the labyrinthine forest. While he slept away the morning, the bamboo was rustling. Lacking the ability to lift his head, Carbie was unaware that he had landed right outside the jungle.

A furry head poked through the bamboo shoots dressed with a top hat. The two hands spreading the shoots wore silky white gloves.

"Hmmm…" the creature said. "What exactly do we have here?"

He smashed through the branches and landed on the soft ground. Carbie awoke, but could only see the damp mud. His body was lifted and draped limply, as a sagging bag of cardboard, over a hairy shoulder. As the transporter moved away from the water, he could see the bamboo shoots close behind, blocking off the tranquil lake. He knew himself to be in a world of trouble, far worse than that of Brimstone's.

DESPITE THEIR FATHER'S misplacement everything in the market was running smoothly. The brothers must have arrived at Havenshaw Crypt in time to deflect the hordes of the dead escaping, for all in the market square were alive and vibrant. The multi-colored tents were just as they'd always appeared, full of a variety of wares and goods.

There was luckily no sign of Lady Moreover or Porticus, but their sentinels marched about the market, wearing sneers and wielding their fanged teeth. They were looking for a reason to cause trouble, trying to seduce the vendors into subservience. One of the dog-faced bastards snapped his teeth at a dealer and came away with a swatch of the blue skinned creature's tissue.

The thing flapped its ears and scaly arms as the guard ripped at its neck. Then, the victim fell behind his wares table, which was covered in oceanic items. The guard selected one of the sale items. The product was alive and kicking its legs as the sentinel held it hostage. He turned in circles, convoking the onlookers.

It barked "You cannot hide such items from our noses. We smell everything. *Everything!*"

Spike couldn't help but feel the statement was pointed at him and Megamouth.

The sentinel cracked the creature in half with his hands and chewed on the fat of the legs. "Golden crab is illegal! This salesman will learn his lesson by the hand of Dictator Porticus. If you're not with him... you're against him and punishment will be dealt out, pitilessly."

The loyalist on his soap box looked directly at Spike and growled. They had been spotted, or more likely smelt. The wolven sentinel dropped to all fours. His armor clanged loudly as he ran at the fugitive pair.

Spike uncurled from Megamouth's waist (they were attempting to remain disguised) and dove at the guard. His metal body clashed with the armor and he bounced like a stray arrow through the market square. His sharp feet stabbed something soft and he wobbled on a horizontal axis. Both of his feet were sticking into the body of an obese Goose merchant.

The bird honked and ran in circles, all the while Spike bounced up and down.

"Holy shit!" it screamed. "I've been *speared* in the chest. Murderer! *Murderer!*"

The goose flew into the roof of his tent and Spike's feet came loose. Spike landed in a pool of sticky liquid. The fat, white blood-dripping bird rose into the air and disappeared through a hole it created with its beak. He looked down. A pile of eggs had smashed under his back and ass. Where was some piss wine when you need it, he wondered.

There were screams and panic, things smashed and crashed against each other. Spike stood. Megamouth was tangled with two sentinels, one in a headlock and the other wrapped over his back, gnawing on his brother's plastic skull. Megamouth slammed his back into one of the tent posts, making the sentinel yelp and the trading posts collapse. Vendors abandoned their tents, leaving the square empty beside the small attacking group of sentinels.

Spike peered down the main aisle of the market. In the center was a giant labyrinth built atop several flights of stairs. The steps wrapped around the sides and ended at the base of the structure. Alleys and tunnels disappeared into the building, pitch black corridors in which one could forever be lost. Several sentinels filed out of the alleys, like a plague of locusts. Spike stretched his arms to full length, making them to resemble fighting sticks.

Megamouth continued to squeeze the sentinel's head until it literally popped off, rolling beneath one of the tables. Rufus became spooked and slid behind the booger-stained handkerchief in Megamouth's chest pocket. A brave but very timid fighter, thought Spike.

Leaving his brother to fend for himself, Spike vaulted into the air. He bent his toes, to dull them, and landed atop the nearest tent roof. The sentinels circled the tent, waiting for him to drop down; they were snarling. When he didn't bite, they used his weakness (family) against him, and raided Megamouth.

After a short struggle with the sentinel on his back, the loudspeaker finally punched one giant fist down its throat. The enemies face split from the corner of his lips to the back of his head. Megamouth yanked his hand out, unfazed, and the body of the sentinel crumpled onto the cobblestones. Without a seconds hesitation he turned toward the oncoming forces. The sentinels did not hesitate either, but viciously tore at Megamouth's suit.

Spike wondered where Rufus was when the time was hot, when Megamouth was in real danger. Then, realized that he was also avoiding the fight, the hypocrite, and Spike was never one to miss combat. Jumping feet first, Spike extended his ten toes into knife-sharp points. One of his legs penetrated a sentinel's stomach, for the armor only covered their head and shoulders, and the other stabbed through another's neck. Two of the sentinels were pinned to the ground, whimpering and convulsing, per order of Spike's pointed feet. He didn't budge from detaining them.

Since Spike was so thin, the wolven minions couldn't get a decent grip on any part of his body. He could feel their jaws wrapping around portions, but it never pained him (not that he really felt pain, anyway). A set of jaws finally clung onto his left limb. With an extended right arm, he beat the beast across the nose until it yelped and loosed its jaw.

They were chewing on Spike's brother, pieces of his suit flying through the air and the sound of teeth on hard plastic ceaseless. Twice Megamouth had rescued him and now Spike needed to save his younger sibling. He jabbed with his longer arm, pushing his fingers into one communal point. The hand penetrated a helmet adorned with an engraving of Porticus Labary and volleyed brain matter into Megamouth's megaphone.

His brother placed two hands over his mouth, gagging back the urge to vomit. Spike covered his ears. When the sound wave rumbled the marketplace, it shot Spike and all of the sentinels flipping through the air in different directions. The pile of glass vases he landed in shattered into thousands of pieces. He stood instantly in a daze and looked around the square. A few of the dog-faced bastards lay in sight, either unconscious or dead. None were erect.

Megamouth wasn't able to withhold and was vomiting onto the cobblestones. Green puke lined the rim of his loudspeaker mouth and chunks splattered everywhere. They were lucky to be alive, but Spike knew if they didn't act quickly then more sentinels and possibly one (or two) of the Five could pose a formidable threat.

"C'mon, puke boy. We gotta' move."

He sprinted past his brother and towards the pyramidal formation. The battle ground for the Dictator's Ball wasn't much farther. Manservant Genesis also lived and maintained the stash of warrior children there. As a team the brothers endeavored there once, immediately preceding the latest years of suspension.

They fought through the surrounding wasteland, killing trolls and smiting centaurs, to get there and before the battle could commence the brothers attacked. They lacked a game plan and, thus, relied upon intuition. Megamouth should have known the final results.

They squared off with Porticus first since appearing behind his throne. However, the other Four were quick to rebuttal. Spike fended off Porticus, going hand to foot with the giant, but the enemy's mind rays were too much for even him. He tried to stab the ten-foot-tall old man, but Spike's actions were under control. His legs carried him to the middle of the coliseum, where children in battle armor beat the shit out of him with maces and battle axes.

Ignatius was fighting Carbie, but really just playing with him, teasing him every step of the way. Brimstone was blasting Megamouth with his flamethrower. Spike could still hear his brother's pain filled screams, battering everyone's eardrums. That's when Manservant aimed his mechanical eye at the small of Megamouth's back and shot the blue laser that caused Spike to lose his cool.

He came free of his hypnotism and began to slice through the children warriors, cutting off heads and disembodying limbs. When his anger subsided, he blasted Manservant with the shadow gun, capturing the bastard. Then, the realization of his actions stung. Despite how against harming children he was, Spike had done exactly the same thing for what the Five were so famously despised. Before he had time to try for retribution or to capture more of the Five, his body was numb and he was magically wrapped around the tree, abandoned to reflect on what he'd done. It was as if father was watching the entire time.

Megamouth brought him out of the reverie. "Is dad in there?" he yelled, pointing at the pyramid they were walking along.

"I'm not sure what is inside there, nor do I care to."

Spike was awful tired. He was tired of questions, tired of looking. His patience was thin. He thought about piss wine and how it could possibly relieve some of the tension, make him forget his troubles. Beyond the square was the jungle, lined with grape vines.

"Do you have my can?" Spike asked. Megamouth offered to shrink it before, so they could travel lightly.

"Yes. One minutes."

He hummed and dug inside of his suit. Rufus came crawling out of the chest pocket and sat on Megamouth's shoulder.

"Hoo-eee!" the little guy said softly. "It's hotter than the inside of a hooker's anal cavity in there!"

He became silent again and Spike wondered his reason for speaking at all. For that to be the first thing he ever heard the thing say was absolutely ludicrous.

"Why didn't you help us out back there?" Spike asked.

Rufus stared at him without saying a word. His lips curled to one side of his light brown face. Spike hadn't noticed before, but the thing had two small horns on his hairline. Then, he whispered into Megamouth's ear. The brother chuckled, but didn't speak. Instead, he pulled out the tool and pressed a button on the side.

The air around the three started to move in suctioning circles and Spike could feel it pulling at his cheeks and arms. There was a deafening growl and his can was sent clanging over the stone walkways.

"Thanks, brother." Spike forgot all about Rufus's obvious snide comments about him and moved toward the jungle to relieve his urge. It was so bad he had to walk with a limp, holding his dangleberry in one hand and the can in the other. He picked as many grapes as possible, dropping them by the handful into the can. It was all he could do to hold back the piss while he stomped the grapes to mush. He needed the piss wine to keep him a level head.

With a sigh he relieved himself. The can filled quickly and he aimed at the crooked bamboo shoots. His head rolled towards his back in supplication as his stream slowed to a pitter-patter. Then, Megamouth started to scream.

Spike bent over and wrapped his dick around his waist. When he turned around eight hairy legs were crawling out the top of the pyramidal structure. They scraped shrilly across the stones, piercingly. Lady Moreover's grey-haired head poked out of the hole and she pulled herself onto the top of the building. Two of the spider legs knit a fine quilt, wantonly weaving in and out of the fabric.

She looked over the crescents of her reading glasses. "Hello, dearies."

Spike squinted and Megamouth cowered. Rufus disappeared into the chest pocket.

"Beautiful day to die, eh?" she asked, and then lunged for Megamouth.

CHAPTER 7

HIS BODY WAS dumped into a pit of sand. He could feel the water seeping out of his body, being absorbed by the grains underneath him. He lay there unattended until finally his arms felt light enough to move and his toes (made of match box pieces) began to wiggle. Carbie stood on wobbly legs. He walked through the sand, sinking from time to time, toward the nearby settlement.

Beyond the shield of bamboo the ancient stone buildings sat dormant, rows and rows of stone huts. They were quite enormous, possibly bigger than Brimstone's elephants. Carbie started through the bamboo and heard a rustling overhead.

He looked skyward. Ignatius the Ape was manipulating his body through the trees. He swung one ape arm over the canopy and a tangle of leaves and sticks came crashing towards Carbie. They broke against his head and body, forcing him to the floor of the jungle. Before he could regain his composure, the ape was upon him, holding his arms close to his body so that they couldn't move.

"I thought that was you." Ignatius closed one eye and eyeballed Carbie from behind a silver rimmed monocle with the other.

"Quite a sorry sack of shit these days, eh?" he said. "Not much for me to worry over."

Holding Carbie like his own personal action figure, Ignatius bounded toward the village. They reached the limits and passed into the open area. Ignatius began to pound the dirt with his free hand.

"People, People!" he yelled in his sophisticate tone. "Please... come and join me for a deliberation of fate. I cannot, and will not, do this by myself."

The random masses started to pour out of their spectacularly built homes. There was a portly family, round and blob-like who barely possessed limbs. They moved in concert, like five jingle bells rolling side by side. A squat Gary ran out of his hut, his curly head of hair bouncing. Something supported by only one leg, which poked out of the center of its torso, sprung up and down towards them.

Ignatius turned in a semi-circle, waving at the motley crowd like a Prince. "Good afternoon, good afternoon."

They formed a line in front of the ape. Carbie was embarrassed by his exposure. The ape held him out for all to see and stare they did. They watched with pleading eyes. He knew they were under control of the monkey-man, wanted Carbie's help for release. They either did what he wished or fell to prosecution, possibly public execution.

"What shall we do with this... scum?" he asked the collective.

The people whispered and murmured about themselves. Carbie could almost feel their reluctance to answer. Then, someone shouted in a high-pitched voice. "Let him go!"

Carbie did not see the culprit and obviously Ignatius hadn't either, for he screamed, *"What?* Who said that hogwash?"

When nobody opened up, the ape waded

through the crowd. Carbie brushed against bodies and they moved away as if he was forged of poison. The ape sniffed the air. Its hot breath played across the back of Carbie's head, smelling of grapes and bananas, the only crops mandated to grow by the dictators.

"You!" One hairy finger pointed over Carbie's shoulder, toward the fat blob father.

"No," he responded. "I did not speak. It was…"

The blob swiveled and found an innocent bystander whose head was shaped like a cube. Initially, its face showed fright, then the head spun to a different side and it was red and angry. The wooden, wiry man attacked the blob without as much as a word. The blob retreated, barely visible feet covered in rolls of fat, carrying it through the dispersing crowd. As he passed, they closed together, making it difficult for the skinny and silent cube-headed man to make progress. However, he eventually freed himself and since the blob moved slowly, was upon his narc in moments. His long arms pounded away at the thing's body. If the blob was able to curl into a ball, it would have.

Carbie was carried out of the crowd. Ignatius pushed the cube-headed attacker to the ground with one ape foot, holding him down. Without any indication of emotion——happiness, anger, mercy, or otherwise——he said "Decision made. *Sentinels!*"

A group of wolven men rushed out of the bamboo. Three pounced on the blob, who was striving to get up off his back. Two more rolled a bamboo cart out of the forest. One of the two wore a hat with a giant red feather. He lifted the door on the cage. "Place them inside!"

They dragged the blob, squealing and whining, and tossed him into the cage. Ignatius used his foot's opposable finger to lift the cube man and toss him head over heels into the trap.

Then, Carbie was turned by the ape to face Ignatius. The ape's large teeth formed a smile. "You, my friend..."

He winked behind his monocle. "I suppose I will add you to my sacrifices. Maybe you'll be killed and I won't have to worry about doing it myself!"

His head rolled back in the most fabricated laughter Carbie ever heard.

"Tough change," Carbie responded, though his lunges felt compressed from the ape's grip. His enemies round eyes came too close for comfort. The monocle pressed against his spandex suit. Then, the ape let out a series of chatters and pounded Carbie against the ground. His head flattened and his thoughts momentarily ceased. When his vision returned, skewed by hanging pieces of his own cardboard head, he could see the obvious leader of the sentinels. It screamed "Fall out!", and the bamboo cart began to roll.

SHE SLAMMED INTO his bulbous body, knitting needles piercing his chest. The mean spider-grandmother pulled them out covered in white plastic, like a knife out of a cake not fully cooked.

Megamouth blasted her with his foghorn. A normal enemy would have been tossed yards away, either dead or unconscious, but Lady Moreover merely scuttled backwards on her eight legs. She jammed the needles into the dirt and steadied herself. Megamouth wobbled forward, but she threw the blanket she'd been knitting over his head.

Spike chugged the rest of his piss wine and dropped the can. As he powered forward, ready to join the fight (hey, who said anything about fair?), she started to knock Megamouth around with the two poles. The behemoth tore at the blanket, trying to rip it off, but it looked as though the fabric had stitched together, wrapping him in a cocoon. His screams were unable to dislodge the cloak.

Megamouth fell to the ground squirming in

panic, and as Lady Moreover jumped in the air——needles poised to stab straight through his heart——Spike turned his hands into ruthless fighting weapons. His pointed fingers curled into claws and caught both of the needles. She pressed with all her insect might, but Spike held his ground.

Looking down at him with her teeth mashed in anger, she no longer resembled a sweet, old grandmother figure, but a murderous clown. She freed one of the needles and with uncompensated speed, swung it in a downward arc. Spike's waist bent at a right angle.

He clawed her varicose vein-covered spider legs, splashing purple blood over the market. Another knitting needle came down on Spike's thighs at an astronomical speed, twisting both of his feet together so that he was crumpled on the ground——just a coil of metal. As if in slow motion, she brought the needle hurtling toward his head. He watched helplessly as it swung downward, inch by inch, and closer by the second to his skull.

Megamouth rushed into his view. Apparently, the spell had worn off the quilt or he'd ripped through it. His plastic shoulder took the brunt of the impact. Something chipped off his neck and went flying. Mega did not voice his pain, but took it out on Lady Moreover, pounding her insect legs with his massive fists, flapping his shit wings until he was at her waist level and shoving one huge hand into her apron covered stomach.

Her arthritic spine cracked and she fell onto the cobblestones. Megamouth did not stop. As she lay there moaning, her knitting needles discarded on the ground, Megamouth mounted her abdomen. He shouted into her face with his megaphone and her head slammed into the stones. It bounced back and Megamouth delivered an onslaught of punches into her wrinkled mug.

Spike tried to shout for him to stop, that Father would punish him, force them both into a state of suspension, but instead felt a grin creep across his face as her legs wiggled in the air. Wrapped in a ball, he could only groan and smile.

Then, Megamouth was weeping and staring

down at what he'd done. "Oh, no!" he sobbed. "Daddy's gonna' be so mad at me! A-huh-huh-huh...I done killt her! I killt her!"

His screams resonated through the market square. Spike wanted to shush him, but couldn't muster the strength to speak. Some piss wine would have been divine, to bring him back to full power. If the sentinels awoke, he thought, they'd be screwed.

Rufus was returned to his shoulder, hugging Megamouth's plastic head and trying to console him. Spike was waiting for the moment where father would catch a metaphysical drift of his brother's miscalculation, the moment he would again be wrapped around the tree on the island (well, maybe somewhere else now that the island was in the middle of Brimstone's forest). When the moment passed, he started to think that maybe Father Necrocious was dead. Perhaps, the Five had done the unimaginable and slain the greatest necromancer to have ever lived.

Megamouth sat on the ground and allowed his arm to hang limply at his side. He had committed the task that Spike yearned to accomplish. There would be no need to discuss it with their father (if he was alive) any longer. The motions were already begun. The Five were reduced to a meager Four.

Spike choked. His small cry finally elicited Megamouth's attention.

"Oh, my brother...so hurt!" he said.

He stood clumsily and walked to where Spike was laying, picked him up into his arms. Though it was difficult to harm Spike, when Megamouth untangled his legs it stung. He nearly howled when his waist was bent into a straight line. Megamouth placed him upright on his feet.

Spike rolled his neck. His head felt like it was going to fall off, but his voice had returned to his throat. "Saved my life again. I really can't believe this shit."

Megamouth squeezed Spike to his breast. "I'm so glad you okay!"

He wiggled out of the hug, never very fond——or comfortable for that matter——with physical contact, unless during combat. Sometimes, he felt it was his only purpose. However, of late, not only was his patience paper thin, but his fighting tactics were inadequate at best.

"Me, too. But we really got to get out of here."

Almost as if his proclamation woke the sentinels, they began to stir. Pieces of armor rose over the flat tabletops.

Megamouth sighed. "Awww…"

He tapped his chest pocket and the contents within shivered. After spreading the pocket away from his body, Megamouth let out a foghorn blast.

Seconds later his tiny, horned daemon, Rufus, crawled drunkenly onto his perch and took a seat.

"What gives?" the creature asked, wobbling as if fresh off an amusement park ride. He twisted one miniscule finger in his right ear.

Megamouth shook his head. "You sleep too much! Now your turn to fight, or else I put you backs in the tool."

The sentinels had since begun their advance and were closing in swiftly. They snarled and shifted, constantly changing formation——first spread out, then in a tight knit group——never quite giving the two brothers or Rufus a point of focus.

The daemon glided off Megamouth's shoulder in a flash of muddled grey. Before Spike could ready for battle, he was in the arms of his younger sibling, smelling those corn and peanut laced wings as they beat the air into his nostrils.

CHAPTER 8

ONWARD TO THE wasteland——the flat landscape covered in black volcanic rock, the flowing rivers of magma, and most worriedly the dancing minions. Some of them were pitch black as the land they protected, nearly blending in, while others were dark yellow and covered in gangrenous lesions. Though Spike told him to fly toward the battleground, his intuition urged him somewhere else entirely. It told him to aim for the western border of the jungle.

He could detect that his brother was mad, but was almost always right with his perceptions. Growing up, father had him place gambling bets at the Marchovie races, because his mind worked in puzzles and general logic. His numbers typically won.

As they flew over the village of stone huts, Megamouth had a fleeting feeling. The town looked deserted, left behind, and creeping through the jungle toward the village were Manservant's wires. They slithered up the bamboo trees, most likely searching for a few final victims to add as pawns in the battle. He steered away from those, for with their proximity an awful cognition had arisen in his chest and tummy.

"Where are you taking us?" Spike asked over the rush, clearly annoyed.

"Me don't know. I thinks that way." His finger pointed toward the wasteland, but in a direction almost on the exactly opposing side of the pyramidal structure and the market square. They'd travelled half the circumference. The coliseum was within miles. Megamouth descended a bit, his sixth sense warning him to do so. He caught a flash of brown through the bamboo below. Something——maybe a rock, maybe an arrow——bounced off his body.

"We under attack!" He screamed. It echoed through the unusually still air.

There was a line of grey and Rufus was back on his shoulder. "Yeesh," he whispered into Megamouth's ear. "Can I take another nap?"

"No, we may needs you!"

He tried to stare into the trees to see the enemy, but from living in Mount Pus, the prolonged exposure to sulfur and other gases had damaged his eyes. With Spike he couldn't let out too loud of a scream, either, for it would brutally harm him.

"Should we fights them?" he asked.

Spike gracefully uncoiled from Megamouth's waist. His eyesight was super adept in comparison, so he peered below at the moving party.

"I want you to let me go, buddy."

"What dew me flys down der next?"

"No, I'm going by myself."

Megamouth squeezed his brother's waist. "I don't want you to gets hurt. Rufus follow you!"

"No, you get to the battlegrounds," he screamed. "Find out what happened to dad and fix this."

Spike dropped through the blue sky like a plunging dart and disappeared amongst the bamboo. Megamouth flapped like crazy toward the coliseum. His brother was the leader and he would listen to Spike. For some reason, though, his intuition was tugging him farther West and not toward the battleground. It was so strong he could not deny it.

Shit wings were definitely his best invention, he thought, for Spike was now walking through thicket and he could pass directly overhead. Plus, if he fell, he only needed to move the fecal wings and he would be saved. They carried him higher into the sky, past the clouds and beyond sight of the ground. As his subconscious made him aware of the height, fright kicked in. He'd never flown so high in his life.

After popping between the clouds, his head knocked into a hard surface. He flipped in the air and

Rufus swung by his lapel, wearing his classic O-mouth. When he righted himself, Megamouth was amazed to see another giant cube, covered in doors. He wondered which one he was supposed to enter and, more importantly, where it would deliver him.

Megamouth tried the knob on the nearest door to no apparent success. The knob didn't feel correct, anyhow. He closed his eyes, granting his brain unremitting control of his body. It guided him to the left, twice swiveling his angle around corners. A powerful wave of energy overwhelmed him. When he opened his eyes, Megamouth beheld a marvelous white door. Though it looked quite plain in comparison to the eclectic assortment that embellished the cube, it felt so wonderful.

The handle was like any other public door handle——vertical, curved, and silver——but the lock was magnificent. Four gears turned against each other while barbs poked out from between the circular mechanism and soft music emanated from the center. Rufus took initiative and jumped onto the lock. The gears immediately swallowed him, mangling his body and drawing him in. Megamouth panicked and tried to grab him, hoping he wouldn't be harmed, but only returned one small red shoe. He started to weep as Rufus completely vanished and he yanked on the door knob with all his might. It would not budge.

Megamouth's body started to drift slowly downward, but as his head dropped below the level of the cube, the white door creaked open. He flapped his wings and rose to enter, relieved to see his small friend intact, a little perturbed, but nonetheless alive and waving him forward. It was bizarre to Megamouth seeing a surface way up in the air, but he didn't debate its existence. He simply walked inside and the door closed behind.

THE TREES JUGGLED his body. His head knocked across the branches and he ultimately fell onto the floor of the jungle on his back. A thick black wire was slithering towards him, shooting sparks out of a stripped end. Spike rolled onto his haunches as the sparking end jabbed at his face. He turned his hand into a straight edge and with one calculated swipe, cut the end off. His action only produced a further frayed tip, which shot more sparks, but the wire slithered away in reverse.

He ran for the shaking bamboo, ahead and to the right. From up in the sky he had seen Carbie in the cage, but hadn't wanted to alarm his emotionally unstable younger brother, seeing as Carbie was hostage to Ignatius the Ape. He also wanted to separate from the hulk in the hopes that if their father was alive, then he would only suspend Megamouth. Unlikely, he knew, but possible.

A boomerang sliced through the bamboo and past his head. He ducked even though it flung to his side. To avoid the enemy in the bamboo, Spike bent his knees and sprang as high as physically possible into the air. He glided above their heads with a smile on his face. This was their terrain, they had home field advantage, and he needed every gag he could pull.

The ground greeted Spike with welcome arms. Though he could hear the sentinels making haste behind him, and he unaware to their sharp teeth right on his heels, he pressed on with passion. His pointed body took flight and his two legs intertwined to form a weapon like a massage octopus. It lopped the head of the rear sentinel off, sending it rolling through the shoots. With his hands, he grabbed ahold of the cart's bars for dear life.

Behind him a dog-faced bastard, trying hard to keep up with the swiftly rolling crate yelled "Intruder!"

The great ape changed direction effortlessly, not stopping for a beat. His massive feet smashed through the cage, making its temporary inhabitants cower flat on the floor with his passing. Spike was kicked in the face and legs at the same time. The top of his head touched the soles of Ignatius's feet and Spike rolled like a pinwheel across the shattered cart's bars.

Luckily his limbs did not bend, but only curved, and he reformed in an instant. A tightly curled fist barely missed him and rumbled the ground.

"Rotten bananas!" cursed the top hat wearing ape.

The creature leaned back on his hands, kicked both feet forward, and Spike fell uniform with the ground. Absolutely nothing could touch him in the position. Then, he performed three consecutive back handsprings and landed on the cart's platform.

His brother was in a heap in the corner. "Carbie, get up!"

The black spandex only sat there, unspeaking. Spike leaned in and heard breathing. "C'mon, get up," he said again, trying to hold his brother together.

As much as he strained, the assassin still fell apart in his arms as disconnected pieces inside a stretchy bag.

"I can't... re-form," he murmured softly.

"That's not possible. You have to."

"No. *I've taken a beating, but I...at least I killed Brimstone.*"

"You did *what?*" Spike asked incredulously.

Carbie mustered a chuckle, "Charred the fucker. Are you so surprised? Go on... get out of here. Keep you and that loudmouth safe. I'm a goner."

Spike was thrown abruptly from the cart, but righted himself to land on his feet. The sentinels surrounded the vessel and the ape hurried upon him. The Flagrant one raked a hair-covered arm through the separating space. Spike bent his body around the attack and parried with a claw to the beast's thigh.

Ignatius screamed out and clapped two hands

together, enclosing Spike. Being pin-thin had its advantage on occasion. Spike slid between the thing's fingers and stood watching the ape look confusedly at both palms. Then, he made his body a missile and launched at Ignatius's uncovered eye.

His feet penetrated with a "squish!" and the monster screeched in agony. The monocle fell from his other eye and dangled like a pendulum. As Ignatius went to place it on, the chain snapped, it fell to the ground, and he accidentally crushed it beneath his foot.

"I'm blind! Blind I tell you!"

Spike pulled his feet out from the enemy's sockets and dropped. If his brothers could destroy a member of the Five and get away with it, then why couldn't he?

The ape fell onto his ass, covering his eyes with his furry hands. "Goodnight, cruel world!" he cried dramatically.

Then, he was still. Spike was sure the fucker would die, if he wasn't dying already, for he'd felt his feet poking into brains. Also sure of the sentinels' forthcoming attack, he turned to continue battle. They were either stunned or frightened because he'd killed their leader, but more importantly Carbie's remains were gone, departed.

He took it as a perfect opportunity to retreat into the bamboo, grabbing a handful of grapes in passing, pissing on them, squishing them, swallowing them, all very proud of himself.

MEGAMOUTH WALKED OVER the light blue dirt, humming. "Dum, da-dum, dum. Dum, da-dum, dum."

He had no clue where he was besides inside

some sort of cubiverse. In spite of the new surroundings, he felt surprisingly comfortable. There was a different sensation to the place, warmer, lighter, like summer all year long. He looked up and the sky was not blue. There weren't any clouds. There was only light blue ground, stretching on a flat plane in all directions forever.

"We're lost aren't we?" Rufus whispered.

Megamouth thought they could be lost, but even so, using his intuition they could be again found!

"I'll get us tos the coliseum. You just wait and c!"

He'd tried to use his shit wings to move them along at a faster rate, but for one reason or another they couldn't take flight. Instead, they walked for hours. At first, Megamouth was concerned with getting to the place Spike told him to reach. However, after a desperately long and sweaty stretch, a spec became visible on the horizon, which stole his focus.

When they were close enough, Megamouth was ecstatic to see his father sitting in his rocking chair. He started to run, but his the chair seemed to be rocking farther across the land.

"Daddy! Daddy!" Megamouth yelled, waving one arm in the air.

"It's an illusion, you idiot," Rufus said. "Someone's fucking with your mind."

Finally, they started to make up ground. The chair, and man, grew larger. He could make out his father's light grey, long hair, his stitched-closed eyelids, and his leathery skin. The old man stopped rocking and leaned forward with their approach.

"My son," he said, holding out both hands. "Come here and give your elderly father a hug."

Megamouth squeezed his father like one squeezes a pet, with equal love and adoration. "We thought you was dead!"

Father Necrocious wiggled out of the grip and sat back down. "Sorry, but you know I must sit. I cannot stand for prolonged periods."

He smacked his rotten teeth together. "There is no death for me. I may go somewhere else, but I'll always be around."

"Me, too?"

"No. Someday you will be gone. Though, when I made you and your brothers I tried to use the most durable materials as possible."

"My brothers! Are they okay?" he asked, knowing his father could see everything.

"Poor Carbie was hurt so badly, I was forced to remold him. Now Spike was fine, but he is a nuisance that one. Unfortunately, they're once more asleep. It had not been my intent to lay them back to rest, for I feel their punishment was well served. Alas, they both killed one of my sons, without remorse. Carbie killed Brimstone in cold blood and Spike murdered my ape-child, Ignatius."

Megamouth was confused, "Da Five your *sons*!"

Necrocious let out a huge sigh. "I created the Five to control the land, but not in the capacity with which they do. Low and behold the power permeated their thick skulls. They started to treat people unfavorably, but I hadn't the heart to destroy them. Then, I created you three to parry their control."

"You don't love us, then? Only made us to fight

big brothers?"

"Sadly, yes, but my love for you three has grown, especially for you. While you may be dim, you have the biggest heart. Carbie and Spike... they lack compassion. You felt remorse for killing my daughter. On the other hand, they felt nothing but a sense of accomplishment.

"Every creature in the world is forged from my hand. Everything alive descends from one of my children. All of them have learned to coexist, but the Five sadly could not. They were not meant to be ruthless leaders. Power overcame their heads and hearts. Of late, their antics have become increasingly worse. I cannot watch my great-great-great-great-great-great, great, great, great grandchildren suffer any longer."

"So everything on this world's my family. I have so many brothers and sisters," Megamouth said proudly.

Necrocious smiled. He tried to open his eyelids. "To protect them you must then capture the remaining Two. The reason I brought you three back, no differently than before, was to capture the Five in their entirety, rid the world of them if even for a short era. I fear they will otherwise contribute to the unmaking of the universe. I wish I did not have to burden you with the task, my son, but only you may *understand.* I do love them, despite their misgivings."

Megamouth did understand. Sometimes people thought he was a dummy, but he wasn't, not always. Daddy loved *all* of his children, even if they were bad, and didn't want to see them hurt. Spike and Carbie wanted to murder them. It was all they knew. Megamouth only killed people when he was forced to, either while working or protecting Spike and Carbie. He decided that after the mission, maybe he would never kill another creature in his life.

"So I go to battle, me and Rufus. No kill, maybe hurt..." he chuckled and his salami-shaped nose wiggled "if me have to. I turn my family to shadows."

Necrocious started to rock. "Good, m'boy. You obey my rules now. When you catch Porticus and Manservant, you bring them to the Crypt. I hope to have everything cleaned up and my other children laid to rest by the time you get home."

"I can stay with you when I get there!" Megamouth shrieked. Luckily, the volume couldn't possibly affect his father's powerful ears.

"It all depends upon you behavior, so good luck and thank you for understanding, son."

He hugged and kissed his father and started to walk in the direction from which they'd arrived.

Rufus whispered "Where in the world does he think we're going to go from here?"

Megamouth shrugged and his father's booming and crackly voice responded. "Your friend is a wise-ass. Have I mentioned that I don't particularly care for him?"

Then, Megamouth's body fizzled into a stream of particles and he felt his existence begin to separate. He was floating through nothingness.

CHAPTER 9

WHEN HE OPENED his eyes, only darkness was visible.

Megamouth worried that his eyes were sewn shut like father's, but after a few minutes shapes began to take form. There were other people standing nearby and he dare not move hastily. He sneakily reached into his pocket and grabbed the multi-tool. Without causing much commotion, Megamouth found the button on the curved part and flipped it up. A blindingly bright light filled the space. There was a scuttling sound and some incoherent (at least to Megamouth) jabbering.

His eyes adjusted to the light and he cried out in fear. The sound was so honest it stuck in the back of his megaphone. They were in between a crowd of standing and sleepy live trolls. The evil beings were in a state of shock and awe, rubbing their bulbous orange eyes and moaning groggily. They were only half the size of Megamouth and covered with hard black scales like roofing shingles.

Megamouth started to move, tip-toeing past the little trolls. "Excuse me," he said as softly as possible.

"Don't fucking talk!" Rufus ordered in a subdued scream.

The Mercenaries Of Havenshaw Crypt

There was no retaliation from the plastic man. He heeded Rufus's warnings and strode in silence. The trolls were like waking babies, babies that for once he did not care to hold or cuddle. Megamouth was waiting for them to start wailing for their mothers in shrill and terrifying voices.

"Careful, careful," Megamouth said, reassuring himself as they started to reach their long clawed fingers toward him. They etched deep cuts into his arms, tearing his wool suit jacket apart. "Times to flies!" he screamed.

His yell cleared a path for lift off. He handed the tool to Rufus, who held it shakily. The light bounced up and down as Megamouth tried to navigate the curving cave corridors. Rocks jutted into his path and he flew either higher or lower to accommodate.

Rufus said "They're gaining on us. Pick it up, loudmouth!"

Megamouth glanced over his shoulder at the risk of crashing. They were very close, almost within reach. When he turned forward again there was a complete blockage. At the last second, he turned left in the hopes of a passage magically being there. He closed his eyes and thankfully continued uninterrupted.

Behind, he could hear bodies slamming into the wall, making splattering sounds. "We's almost out!"

Ahead there was a small circle of light, which grew wider every second. Megamouth could discern the solid black ground outside of the cave. So close... so close... so close... something snagged his foot.

The duo went hurtling out of the cave. Megamouth looked at his foot and was taken aback. One of the midget trolls was latched onto his pants leg and was chewing away at his foot. Half of his ankle was completely gone.

Rufus opened the multi-tool. A giant racket fell out and he began to swing it at the clinger. It wouldn't let go and Megamouth started to shake his leg.

"Get off, get off."

His daemon smacked the troll in the face. It hissed and then fell into a stream of magma. Hordes of demons rushed out of caves——yellow, green, orange—

—and all reached out to grab them. Then, a group of purple demons with scabbed wings appeared.

Each demon grabbed the legs of the preceding, forming a giant flying serpent. The creation swung in fluid movements, back and forth, back and forth, whipping demons toward the pair. Megamouth panicked and bee lined for an aged stone tower, aiming for the window near the top.

A fat red troll with a fuzzy head of hair popped out of the window. Between his pointed teeth, he said, "come to poppa'!"

As an alternative, Megamouth flew around the left side and slanted right, coming almost full circle around the tower. The serpent curved around both sides, but broke off into two separate trains. He howled with his foghorn and sent one of the snakelike groups into the side of the tower, smashing the demons like insects across the stone. The other serpent directed for them and Megamouth stopped flapping. They dropped instantly, but were grabbed out of the air by a pair of hands.

"Mine, mine," the creature said. It was a red troll, possibly the one from the other window, who was bigger and stronger than Megamouth.

"Please let us go," Megamouth pleaded. He couldn't fight back, for the demon had wrapped around his legs, arms, and torso.

"No way. I'm gonna' have fun with you."

Something hard and rod-like poked into Megamouth's leg. With limited options, he shoved his salami nose into the red troll's yellow teeth. The thing released them when his front teeth cracked out of his gums, and Megamouth fluttered out of the window.

A lava fountain exploded directly across the way and when the exhibit cleared, he could see the coliseum waiting beyond. Megamouth flapped harder than he had in his whole life. A purple demon latched onto his pants leg. They were much bigger than the black trolls and weighed him down. It started to climb his body, carrying with it the ten or so demons trailing behind, latched to its legs.

He flew over the wall of the coliseum. Three of

the thrones around the top of the stands were empty and the stands full of patrons, the battle in progress. The painted children were clashing, steel connecting with steel.

Megamouth could feel the demon on his lower back. He looked for Porticus while at the same time digging for his shadow gun. The old man was close by, his eyes closed, rocking back and forth like father, obviously directing his psychic attack. Part of Megamouth's shit wing broke off and along with it went the string of demons. He and Rufus began to descend at a rapid rate. Megamouth pulled out his shadow gun, pointed it toward Porticus, and compressed the trigger. His brother's eyes shot open.

Porticus's grey hair became a wave as he did a back flip to avoid the ray. The crowd cheered when he landed on his feet, perched on the rim of the coliseum. Despite their awful ways, the Five (or Two) had loyal followers. Porticus bent his brittle knees, ready to spring. His jeans ripped and he tumbled forward. Megamouth again pulled the trigger.

As his body somersaulted forward, Porticus warped, turning pitch black. His jeans were swallowed by the shadows, his button-down work shirt engulfed by the darkness. The silhouette was sucked into the gun.

They were barely buoyant——Megamouth flapping his one shit wing, Rufus waving the racket too large for him to hold——when Megamouth noticed Manservant. He was crouched on his throne, pointing his eye laser directly at them. Without giving Mega a second to react, the blue laser sliced through the stadium. Megamouth could smell burnt shit as they fell.

He tried to brace for the landing by bending his knees, but when he hit the half-chewed leg shattered and he crumpled to a heap. The painted children fell on him, wielding weapons, covered in war paint, and started to destroy his torso. His chest cracked in half, screams encompassed him, and his other leg shattered into shards. Rufus dropped the multi-tool and vanished inside the chest pocket. A high-pitched whine rang out and all the children stopped, whimpering and covering their ears. The loud footsteps could only come from one person.

Sure enough, Manservant stood over them, his body covered in metallic green armor, wires covering his arms and body. A series of computerized beeps came out of his mouth like Morse code. It translated as a fluorescent scroll across the backdrop of the coliseum's walls.

"YOU FOOL."

Along the upper rim of the coliseum, massive wires started to slither, blocking anyone's exit.

"YOUR DUTY IS NOW TO ME. I, DICTATOR, WILL ALWAYS BE THE LEADER OF THIS MISERABLE REALM. EVEN WHEN I'M GONE THERE WILL BE ANOTHER TO TAKE THE REIGNS. I REPRESENT ONLY ONE OF A GROUP WITH THE SAME IDEALS."

Megamouth reached for the multi-tool and Manservant poised the laser at his face. He went to press the button for the tool's shield, but accidentally pressed the wrong one.

"Yuh-oh."

The laser melted the left side of Megamouth's

face and his vision depleted. Glass shattered and out of the corner of his right eye, Megamouth saw his germ wing collection escape into the atmosphere. He pressed another button and the rectangle shield spread over his body. Blue light bounced off the translucent shield and hit Manservant in the evergreen suit of armor.

His rounded, helmeted head gagged forward over and over. The germ wings invaded his lungs. Both of his hands, covered in multi-colored wires, clung to his throat as he gasped for life. He bent over and fell out of Megamouth's sight.

The children were coughing as well, dying. The wires started to creep inside the stadium. Megamouth felt the individual pieces of his body go numb.

"What have I did?" he said.

The fragments of his megaphone connected into one uniform cone directly on his face. The smithereens of his body miraculously merged. Then, he evaporated into thin air.

CHAPTER 10

"MY CHILDREN ARE SLEEPING, there's little to do. I'm blinded darkness, my vision askew."

The rocking chair squeaked in the desperate silence of the wooden shack. Father Necrocious, for once in his life, felt at peace. It'd been a long time since last he was able to pursue actual rest. His candle burnt out, the smell of flames gone from the singular room. The ones belonging in the crypt were laid down eternally.

He knew Megamouth killed Porticus by accident. Maybe if he behaved long enough at Mount Pus, then Megamouth could return to Havenshaw Crypt and they could live at home together...maybe.

A shadow slinked past Necrocious's back. He ceased rocking and leaned forward in his chair, lighting a match and moving it nearer to the worn out, blackened candlewick.

"Shhhh..." he said, bringing a long withered finger to his wrinkled lips.

The shadow faded into a darkened corner.

"My children are sleeping, there's little to do. I'm blinded by darkness, my vision askew."

The Father began to ease the chair forth and back, forth and back. He tried to reason with the Sandman, but the shadows were non-compliant, in a constant state of motion.

"Time for more children," the old man said and grabbed for the decanter resting on the round mahogany table.

END.

D.G. Sutter is the author of *La Maquina Oscura* and the collection *Oddly Chilling*. His short fiction has appeared both online and in several small press print anthologies. When not writing he can be found on the North Shore of Massachusetts, fighting the cruel Atlantic with his fishing pole. Keep up with him at www.dgsutter.wordpress.com.

Also available from ~MorbidbookS~

In Print & Kindle Editions:

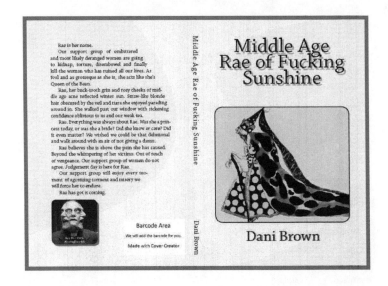

Rae is her name.

Our support group of embittered and most likely deranged women are going to kidnap, torture, disembowel and finally kill the woman who has ruined all our lives. As foul and as grotesque as she is, she acts like she's Queen of the Bean. She walked past our window with sickening confidence oblivious to us and our weak tea.

Rae believes she is above the pain she has caused. Beyond the whimpering of her victims. Out of reach of vengeance. Our support group of women do not agree. Judgement day is here for Rae.

Rae has got it coming.

"No! You will not move. You say I am a fucking clown, and so I will be. And I will fuck you until I can fuck you no more. And when I am done, perhaps I will take you down to the cattle car and watch while the other clowns fuck you one by one until you are so full that their juices run down your thighs. You will learn to show respect for me. For my art and my craft."

Pinning her hands to the bed, he entered her quickly and roughly. She screamed and spit in his face. He slapped her again and left her ear ringing.

"You hate clowns? A fucking clown is raping you and he'll continue to do it until it pleases him to stop."

Vengeance of
the Vigilante
Roller Sluts
~SK8orDIE~

GREGOR COLE

~The hands of the girls were inside of each-others zip front grey boiler suits and they sat in the blood from where Sonny's face collided with the surface. The brunette had a finger smear of it next to her mouth.

"You two sluts put each other down and go tell Moira that Sonny's done. I'm coming in, just got a little business to attend to first."

As the two started to leave the big blond grabbed the shoulder of the red head and pulled her back.

"Not you Fire-Crotch, all this fucking blood has got me going." She started to unbuckle the belt on her camouflage hot pants. "Down you go, bitch!"

~**Short stories from the Most Depraved Writer in Print.** Dark and twisted tales of exquisite violence, rough tricks, narcotics consumption, evil ghosts and drug-snuffling demons. Evil grandfathers and animal-human hybrid clones. Morbid serial killer stalking night darkened hallways of an unsuspecting hospital. Life underground following the frozen apocalypse. Tales of ancient blood-thirsty vampires and Roman decadence. Enjoy all of the hardcore, dystopic, viscerally violent stories. Not for easily offended mamby-pambies. Dark fiction at its finest.

The Mercenaries Of Havenshaw Crypt

~From Alex S. Johnson, the author of Bad Sunset, Wicked Candy and The Death Jazz, comes a new vision in Bizarro horror. Imagine a TROMA film on meth and acid, one part cyberpunk, one part Franz Kafka, and three parts frankly unsuitable for a sane audience. "Will make you feel as if you've just eaten 8 Percocets and washed 'em down with a bottle of moonshine," says Necro Stein of Texas Terror Entertainment.

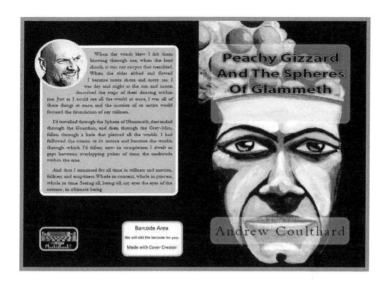

~**When the winds blew i felt them blowing through me,**
when the land shook, it was my corpus that trembled. When
the tides ebbed and flowed I became more shore and more
sea. I was day and night as the sun and moon described the
steps of their dancing within me. Just as I could see all the
world at once, I was all of these things at once, and the
motion of an entire world formed the foundation of my
stillness.

I'd travelled through the Sphere of Glammeth, descended
through the Guardian, and then through the Grey-Man,
fallen through a hole that pierced all the worlds.

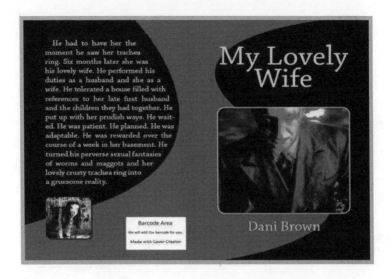

~He had to have her the moment he saw her trachea ring. Six months later she was his lovely wife. He performed his duties as a husband and she as a wife. He tolerated a house filled with references to her late first husband and the children they had together. He put up with her prudish ways. He waited. He was patient. He planned. He was adaptable. He was rewarded over the course of a week in her basement. He turned his perverse sexual fantasies of worms and maggots and her lovely crusty trachea ring into a gruesome reality.

~A dirty shameful devil of a secret...

Something that two men share. A legacy that will shock you to your very core. One that is created not out of madness, but of the purest desire. Take a vivid journey into the mind of the killer and his biggest fan. Do you believe in evil? See the knife plunge. Lap at the wounds. Do you still? There is no rational meaning or pretty words that will hide away the darkness that the words of this found journal creates. Inside is the real truth. And it can set you free. Watch all you want. Taste what you dare not have.

~"**The routine has this inherent tendency to perpetuate lies,**
and I speak only in thinly veiled euphemisms — hanging out
with friends means going to the bar; being tired means too
many sleepless nights on amphetamine; going grocery
shopping means robbing Price Chopper blind; filling a
prescription means visiting my dealer; going to the bank
means pawning my possessions — but refer to them not as
"lies;" rather, label them as weak excuses utilized to justify my
erratic behaviours.

~**I'm feeling down and dirty, feeling kind of mean,** so I give those fans my middle finger. Those poor bastards go nuts. My team looks at me in awe. My coach frowns and the opposing one begins to furiously scratch out new plays. I see our opponents and I almost feel sorry for the poor bastards. Their fans can't help them. Their coach can't help them. I'm going to run them off their own track in front of their own fans and there is not one thing they can do about it.

The Mercenaries Of Havenshaw Crypt

~**Humanity is the devil is a deconstructed nightmare mixing David Lynch and snuff movies.** The plot revolves around a central character, Seth, who is set about a crusade against humanity which, for him, represents pure evil. Through random killings he and his cronies try to accelerate the end of the world, in order to provoke and defeat the Demiurge, the false God that is ruling the earth. As in Burroughs, logical language is replaced here with cut-scenes – sometimes to be taken literally – that plunge the reader into an extreme experience.

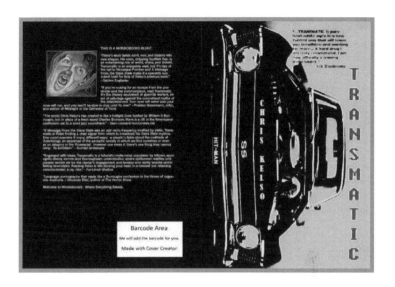

~"As a part-time hitman/ exterminator, Ignius Ellis's dream is to buy a candy-apple red Nova Supreme. In the process of trying to earn enough cash to make his dream come true he gets sucked into the rough world of Visitacion Valley, SF. When the tenants in his apartment complex reveal their various extracurricular activities this take an even more bizarre twist and Ellis soon becomes acquainted with the nightmarish Slave State dimension..."

~That's the last time she gets the bigger worm...

Once their flesh flakes away the angels collapse into puddles of hissing goop and withered petals blow into them hurried along by unseen winds. My spit looses its sweet taste to the black flavor of ash. The glowing birds in the bright orange sky burst into small sparkly novas. The sky itself weeps and tears, streaking down like a ruined painting as the dismal grey of life wheezes back before my eyes. I don't blink; praying silently for one last desperate sensation of the high. Lila feels it too. She writhes on the mattress next to me...

~Scary as ever.

He looked at her and grinned wickedly, the overcasting shadows of the outer corner of the stone wall, combined with the flickering light above them, created a deadly feature across the side of his face. He sees her lying helpless. He chuckled eerily, and instantly raised his hand. Her eyes widened to the sight of the gleaming sharp knife in his grasp. He even held it up for her to see it better.

She stared up at him and then to the knife, panting in fear. Her heart pounded throughout her body as he chuckled once more saying deeply,

"Oh excellent. I've found you . . ."

The Mercenaries Of Havenshaw Crypt

~**Within these twisted and perverted pages,** Johnson manages to demolish clichés with a jaded finesse that I've personally never encountered in written form. Another apparent talent is his effortless deconstruction of pop-culture allegories and references as found in his story "Vampussy." No one is safe or spared from his dagger sharp sarcasm and wit.

While not without its flaws, my appreciation for this kind of talent and voice is what made his writing so fun to read, even if he might possibly be out of his ever-loving mind.

~In Garrett Cook's Murderland serial killers are idolized by society. Their deeds are followed obsessively by television pundits and the adoring public. A subculture has grown up around this phenomena, called "Reap." Laws are created to allow this activity to flourish, including designated "safe zones' where killers can practice their trade without fear of persecution. Fans of the top rated serial killers celebrate each new kill on social media and television. Programs glorify their deeds.

The culture of Murderland is violent and mirrors our own violent society and its decadent obsessions.

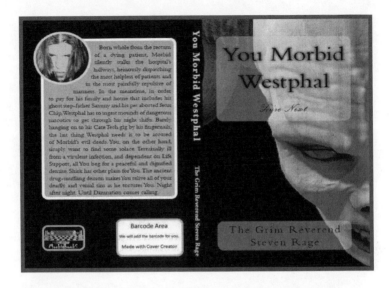

~Born whole from the rectum of a dying patient, Morbid silently stalks the hospital's hallways, heinously dispatching the most helpless of patients and in the most painfully repulsive of manners. In the meantime, in order to pay for his family and home that includes his ghost step-father Sammy and his pet aborted fetus Chip, Westphal has to ingest mounds of dangerous narcotics to get through his night shifts. Barely hanging on to his Care Tech gig by his fingernails, the last thing Westphal needs is to be accused of Morbid's evil deeds. You, on the other hand, simply seek some solace from all Your diseases.

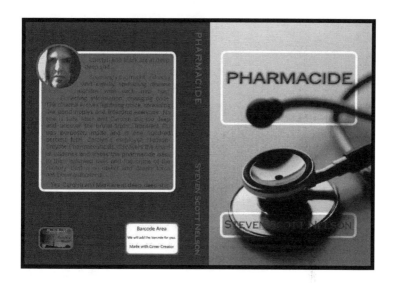

~It looks like Carolyn and Mark   are in deep, deep shit...
Mark and Carolyn live in an alternate 1989 where Ronald
Reagan is on his fourth presidential term. The USA has a
rigid, long-standing caste system and abortions were never
made legal. Being homeless is a crime that is punishable by
imprisonment in Tent City. Most of Mark's ER patients are
inmates at this camp and are victims of a new disease
dubbed: Transient Flu. This deadly and rapidly spreading
disease mutates with each new host, collecting information,
changing code. The disease evolves lightning quick,
spreading like pond ripples...

The Mercenaries Of Havenshaw Crypt

~IMMANUEL THE CHRIST has some nerve. Jonah has already lost everyone he loves to Pilate the vampire and his Harbor drug violence. Jonah now trudges through his days staying as high on Plata as possible. He just wants to be left alone while he waits for his turn to die. The Christ has other plans for him. She sends Pedro, to assign Jonah to order the Herod to dismantle the Harbor's Plata trade. Jonah decides to run. But you can't run from God. As Jonah learns the hard way when the 'Edmund Fitzgerald' goes down in rough seas, with the reluctant prophet on board…

~**Five Very Wicked Shorts**. Brought to you with love and blood from The Grim Reverend Steven Rage, the 'Most Depraved Writer in Print'. ~

Through the sheer shock of his presentation, Rage forces readers to consider the alternatives, to look at the garbage in the streets, to see what is swept into the gutters at night right before all decent people awake to see another cleaned up version of the day. Depravity at its finest, but really the stories are loads of fun.

The Mercenaries Of Havenshaw Crypt

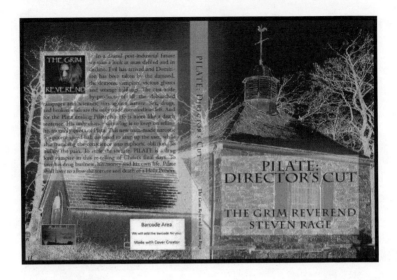

~**Pontius Pilate is cursed to be a vampire.** Life after life after life.~ And for the Plata dealing Pilate, his life is more like a death sentence. His only chance surviving is to keep on selling his monthly quota of Plata. This new man-made narcotic is a potent speed-ball designed to amp up the user, while also numbing the conscience into euphoric oblivion. To nullify the pain. To stifle the torture. To run and to hid from all the anguish inside. PILATE is a drug lord vampire in this re-telling of Christ's final days.

~So I, The Spun Monkey, have returned from running my errands, safe and sound. Having failed rehab once again, The Spun Monkey went ahead and procured myself an 8-ball of crispy, crunchy Columbian Bam-Bam. I chipped, chopped, lined and blasted off with two bigguns up each side. OOH OOH EEE EEE-fuckmerunning- OOH-OOH-OOH, motherfuckers! Monkey be ready... Yes, indeeeeeed.... Having had my jet fuel, I then sat my hairy asshole down at the keyboard and began flailing away. The monkey hopes you dig the fruits of my labors in 'The Spun Monkey's Digest'. And if you not ... well then ... you can go eff yourself, Capitan!

~**Following religious folklore, parables, and beliefs,** Rage presents the readers with a God who truly is the Shepherd that leaves no sheep behind. While this tale is deeply woven with the intricacies of a dark, drug-infested world ruled by evil forces, this is the story of a lost sheep. All are God's children, even the most foulest of evil creatures who by their own will have become so through their spiritual and physical copulation with the Devil, and as such, in God's mercy, still are given a chance to be saved.

~ CARGO CONTAINS: ~

Space-wrecked on Venus by Neil R. Jones

For All the Marbles by Rev. Steven Rage

Tony and the Beetles by Philip K. Dick

Acid Bath by Vaseleos Garson

The Butterfly Kiss by Arthur Dekker Savage

The Moon Destroyers by Monroe K. Ruch

From some of the giants of the Golden Age to the darkest of dystopian noir, MorbidbookS SciFi Anthology will take you from hopeful space travel to living hand-to-mouth in the despair beneath the Earth.

Welcome to your future.

The Mercenaries Of Havenshaw Crypt

~During the height of England's Bubonic Plague an ancient Evil Force strolls into London-Town in the form of a would-be doctor. It could smell the blood from miles away, wanting only to help. At the hospital where he cares for the victims of this Black Death, the ill come to him unimpeded. They arrived and fell by the scores. With the help of his ever-faithful assistant, Sightless Agnes, a most ravenous cares for them all. Eating his way through an entire hospital, he treats them until there is nothing left. Nothing save their empty eye sockets, a few pounds of leeched bleached bones and some bolts of old dried-out flesh-leather parchment.

~New from MorbidbookS; Where Everything Bleeds is an instant collector's specimen and a certain stunner. ~ Be the first freak on your block to acquire this singular and unexpurgated exquisite culling of The Grim Reverend Steven Rage's favorite 'meds'. Enjoy this one–of–a–kind vivid look into the twisted mind of The Most Depraved Writer In Print as he captains you through the intoxicating stain of his wicked imagination. Included are numerous Photos, Paintings and Illustrations embellished with dramatic grayscale that enhance these iniquitous and magnificent Dark Fantasy fables.

MorbidbookS. Everything Bleeds.